M. Reed

Also by Cydney Chadwick:

Enemy Clothing
Dracontic Nodes
The Gift Horse's Mouth
Oeuvres (reprinted as Sleight of Fancy)
Persistent Disturbances
Interims
Inside the Hours
Persistent Disturbances (revised edition)

Benched

Cydney Chadwick

Pivotal Prose Series

Avec Books

Prefatory Note

In the summer of 1999 I asked Gad Hollander, an American poet and filmmaker who lives in London, if he would check the accuracy of the British English I use in this novella, and the London locales—the latter of which I constructed from memory. After reading it he remarked that he'd written a prose piece that had a superficial resemblance to mine called *Benching with Virgil,* where the opening of the narrative takes place on a bench. Neither of us had, of course, seen each other's texts. I wanted to publish both works in tandem as I liked how different prose narratives that include activity on benches (or lack thereof), can be. In thinking further about publishing them, I decided to start a new imprint of Avec Books called the Pivotal Prose Series, dedicated to shorter books of innovative prose. I am proud to announce that an excerpt from Mark Wallace's novel, *Dead Carnival,* will also be published in this series, but it does not contain any benches.

—*C.C.*

Thanks to Mark Wallace for his editorial suggestions regarding this book, and thanks to Gad Hollander for his help with London locations and my usage of British English.

ISBN:1-880713-23-3

Library of Congress Control Number: 00-13441

©2000 by Cydney Chadwick

Cover photograph by Andrew Bick

Cover design by Colleen Barclay

First Edition

All rights reserved

The Pivotal Prose Series
is an imprint of Avec Books
P.O. Box 1059
Penngrove, CA 94951

Contents:

1.
≈
11

1.
≈
29

1.
≈
41

1.

THE MAN ONCE had power and prestige in his life, had both economic and community status, and with it came many friends, many admirers. But he made some bad decisions, wound up losing a great deal of his money, his power, and most of his friends.

The man does laundry. He sits on a bench. He writes down telephone messages for his wife, and tries new recipes for the evening meal. His cooking improves as his good humor declines.

He isn't sure what to do—and knows he can't do much, so during the laundry's drying cycle, he goes to his bench with a notebook and composes a list.

He begins to save the allowance his wife allots him, and when he has enough, hurries to a call-box and begins dialing the numbers he has written down. No one is home at that time of day, but he puts on his most jovial voice to leave his messages, asking if the person would like to get together sometime. If the woman does, she is to return his call on Tuesday through Thursday, between 9:05 a.m. and 2:45 p.m. However if he is not in, she *may not* leave a message; if someone other than himself answers, she is to pretend she is a telemarketer; calling on a bank holiday is out of the question.

In his house the dryer comes to a halt and the warm, fluffy clothes lie still as he finishes his last call and slowly walks back across the park.

When the women return home from work in the evening they play their messages or access their voice mail, listen to the man's proposal and laugh, thinking it is some sort of joke, that they must really make more of an effort to stay in touch with old acquaintances—and promptly forget about the calls. Some of the spouses or boyfriends of the women mumble something about a weird message that was left—

it sounded like a nutter, and how did he ever get their numbers?

A recipient of one of his calls, who is as lonely and bored as the man, gets in touch at one of the appointed times. He is very happy to hear from her and names a fashionable place near the park to meet.

He greets her on the restaurant's stairs, and the woman is shocked by his appearance: his clothes are stained and dirty, and as he embraces her, she is aware that he has not bathed.

He takes her arm and escorts her into the foyer, leaves a false name with the hostess and launches into a diatribe about how the establishment would have a much larger profit margin if there were a neon sign marking its locale. He begins to describe what the sign might look like. A queue forms behind him, of which he is unaware. Startled and concerned, the woman steps away from the queue, bows her head and tries to decide if there is time to say she is not feeling well and must leave immediately, but there is not.

When they are seated they note the changes in one another. Each decides the other looks a little worse for wear, accordingly redouble their efforts to seem excited and enthusiastic. The man happily calls her attention to his bell-bottom trousers, which he has had since the 1970s and has slimmed down enough to be able to include, once again, in his wardrobe—this followed by a suggestion that they drink alcoholic beverages. The woman can think of no reason to decline.

When the man is sure the libations have had an effect, he makes his move—encouraging her to present a paper at a conference on a subject about which she has little knowledge. He has seen her name on a conference advertisement. When she explains that she really has no expertise on that subject, she remembers that *he*, in fact, does. He brightens ever so slightly as she recalls this.

For the remainder of the reunion, the man flares his nostrils at certain things the woman says, to impart that they are a bit too unconsidered and *facile*. Over a brandy he makes subtle but derogatory comments about the woman's last two books.

After lunch the man wants to go for a short walk in the park. She notes the pleasure he derives from asking a classmate of his daughter, whom they come upon, a question about British foreign policy, and his amusement when the girl, unaware she is being mocked, splutters while trying to express herself.

He says it is getting late, that he must go and shop for his family's evening meal, but that he had a nice time, and would like to meet again someday.

o

The woman is on the Circle Line feeling melancholy and confused. She is disturbed, saddened by the man's appearance—that he seems to have lost a good deal of interest in living, and yet appeared to derive a great deal of pleasure from berating her. She remembers hearing several years previously that something had happened to him, something about bad investments, followed by a scandal involving a student, followed by a marital separation. Of course she would never have asked him about these things, and he hadn't brought them up himself.

She also got the impression that he was pretending it was fourteen years earlier, when he was at the pinnacle of his career and she was a graduate student.

o

The woman decides to forget about the strange meeting with her old friend. People change, after all, and he isn't the only person from her past with whom she has met up with in recent years, only to be made unhappy or alarmed. Other encounters have made her wonder what ever brought her and this person from her past together in the first place, and which one of them had changed so radically.

She corrects papers, shuffles around in her slippers, and looks out the window of her flat at the rain, dreading the days she must go in and teach at university. She often has the urge to say while in front of a group of indifferent-looking students: *Fuck it. None of you are going to remember any of this in a year's time, or even six months' time—and you don't care if you do, and I've talked myself in to not caring, so let's just fuck-it-all and go home.* But of course she does not. Instead, she redoubles her efforts, tries to make the material as palatable and interesting as possible, to show it has relevance in their lives, yet week after week she is met with their vacant gazes.

The woman is surprised to hear from the man again five days later—from another call-box, this one in High Holborn; he would like to rendezvous on a bench in the park, near the Serpentine. He tells her his schedule is busy, and it is easier for him to walk over to the park for an hour or so. He also says he has no money for lunch and slams down the phone. She frowns at the receiver before slowly replacing it; she never agreed to meet him, his number is not listed, and now she has no way of reaching him to say she doesn't want to.

The woman races out of the underground and toward the bench where the man is supposed to be. She sees him there, alone, watching the ducks. It occurs to her that he looks like a Beckett character, disheveled, disgruntled and sad.

The man is eating curry from a white paper bag and when she sits down he hands her another white bag containing chapati, dal and a samosa; he hopes she likes Indian takeaway. As they perspire over their lunches, he tells her it is as if he has died: he sometimes sees his former colleagues in the shops, or at a film, and they look startled, as if they are surprised he is still living. She says it must be his imagination. He shakes his head, offers her a napkin to wipe her forehead, and tells her there are certain things about her appearance she could improve, perhaps she might lighten her hair several shades, and get contact lenses. A piece of samosa nearly falls out of her mouth, which she covers with her hand when she starts choking. He pulls her hand away from her face and takes it in his. *Remember when you were in love with me?*

She is upset. She is on the Piccadilly Line glowering at a man in a business suit who is deliberately sitting too close to her, hoping to rub against her leg. This is not what is bothering her, however. She is distressed about her friend on the bench. He has obviously gotten her mixed up with someone else. She was never in love with him, nor he with her. They were friendly, and he admired her work, or at least seemed to. She wonders if perhaps he has gotten her confused with that student, the one involved in the scandal.

She is tired of the businessman being so close to her and abruptly gets up, moving several seats down. Several elderly women sitting opposite them who saw the entire thing are now glaring at the businessman who retreats behind a newspaper. The woman gets off at Russell Square, and goes into the university library. There she begins to look up neurological diseases, and although she is certain she will remember what she reads, she makes notes in a notebook, thinking they might be of some use.

Atherosclerosis: a disorder of large and medium-sized arteries, most commonly the large coronary arteries that supply the heart muscle with oxygen-rich blood. . .it results in a decrease in smooth blood flow and may ultimately deprive a vital organ, such as the heart or brain, of its blood supply. . .

Stroke, also known as cerebrovascular accident (CVA), involves damage to the brain because of impaired blood supply and causes a sudden, nonconvulsive malfunction of the brain. . .

Parkinson's disease or parkinsonism, is a chronic disorder characterized by involuntary tremulous motion beginning in the hands at rest. Movements become slow as the muscles become rigid, causing a masklike face, and the torso tilts forward . . .

She puts her notebook back in her purse, extremely discouraged. While they were at lunch she noticed the man's hands trembled; she also recalls that when he was teaching he always had a lit cigarette in his office ashtray, was very fond of lunching on meat pies and stopping off at the pub when his day was done. The information on atherosclerosis stated that alcohol consumption, cigarette smoking and high cholesterol are contributing factors. If the man is suffering from one of these diseases, or has suffered a slight stroke, wouldn't his family have noticed? But perhaps they do know, and that is why he has been relegated to the position of a domestic servant.

o

I'm at King's Cross. Please come meet me. He is calling at an unusual time, early evening. She is correcting half-term essays and decides she could use a break. The woman puts on her outdoor clothes and meets him twenty minutes later. He takes her arm, leads her down the street and up some stairs. It seems to be the back entrance to a series of very dingy hotel rooms. She pulls away. *Don't worry, I no longer have any interest in that.* He unlocks the door, steps inside and turns on a small black-and-white television. He removes his clothing and gets into bed. She stands in the hallway, gaping. He turns toward her and says in a friendly manner: *Come in. You're getting the wrong idea.* He is hardly a physical threat, and partially out of curiosity, partly out of confusion, she goes into the room, closes the door behind her and sits on a chair near the small vanity table. When the television is warmed up she sees the program *Master Mind* is on and the former professor plays along, answering most of the questions correctly. He looks over to her: *Kind of like the old days,* he says, *or rather, it isn't,* and refocuses his attention on the game, while the woman sits immobilized with shock and astonishment, unable to decide how to react.

o

It is raining. It has been raining all morning, but he hasn't called to change the meeting place. She thinks the rain implies their meeting is cancelled, but as she is unable to get in touch with him to confirm this, she goes to the park in her rain attire, concluding that this is really the most annoying situation. Mercifully, he is not on the bench. Still, she has taken the trouble to come all the way over on the underground in this foul weather. There is a sandwich shop further along. She'll get a sandwich, go back to the flat and get more work done.

I thought you would know to come here. He waves to her from a small table as she stands in the doorway of the shop, her Wellingtons and anorak dripping onto the linoleum floor. *It is too bad you're late...and wet.* She was expecting to eat her sandwich alone. He pulls a chair out for her in an exaggerated manner. He wants to talk about the conference. He has heard from a former colleague that the paper she gave went over extremely well. He is tense, upset: *Don't think you're all that successful,* he admonishes. *You're only a junior lecturer, and you haven't published in the really important journals!* He finishes the sentence in a high, jubilant tone.

She slaps her sandwich down in the middle of the table, gets up, throws on her rain slicker and walks out the door.

o

The woman is screening her calls. Since the day she dashed out of the sandwich shop someone has been calling, getting her answering machine and hanging up. She suspects it is her former professor, but she can think of no reason why she should converse with him—his behavior has become so strange—hostile, unpredictable. And she is fairly certain he still believes she is someone else.

o

It is spring. The woman has joined a health club near Hyde Park that gave her a free introductory offer. After lifting weights, she and several women she's met there have begun to jog around the park in fair weather. Today the sun shines and the woman who is the fastest leads them toward the Lido. As they run down the path near the Serpentine, they pass the man on his bench. He is speaking to a woman seated next to him. She continues jogging with her group and does not acknowledge the man, nor does he acknowledge her. She has not thought of the man since that winter, when the hang-ups on her answering machine finally stopped.

The woman develops tendonitis in her knee. A fitness consultant at the health club shows her exercises to do on one of the weight machines to alleviate it, advises her to treat the knee with ice until it is healed, and to refrain from jogging.

As she cannot run, she now walks in the park, since it is the only time she ever gets out of doors. Because it is so close to the health club, she likes to take advantage of Kensington Gardens' and Hyde Park's meandering paths. She has walked rapidly by the man several times. He seems oblivious to her, or else he has decided to behave as if he were oblivious to her. He is usually seated with a woman. Each one, she notes, is progressively younger, and it is never the same woman twice. On a Saturday afternoon when she finishes correcting papers and has nothing much to do, she decides to go to the health club, then for her stint in the park. She spies the man sitting on the bench near the Serpentine. He is with a group of young girls. She creeps up behind them and places her foot and arms against a tree, pretending to stretch her calf muscle. He is reading something to them, and as she tries to make out what, she observes that one of the bored-looking girls is his youngest daughter, much older now than when a photograph he once showed her was taken. What he is reading is familiar to the woman, but she cannot recall where it is from. Finally she recognizes that it is the most well-known book he ever wrote, published sometime in the early or mid-1960s. The girls' legs dangle from the bench and they kick one another for something to do.

o

Finally, summer weather. The woman's knee has healed and she has resumed jogging. Marches are being played by a military police band on the bandstand in Kensington Gardens, the music growing fainter as she crosses the street that leads into Hyde Park. As she rounds the path toward the Serpentine she looks over at the bench. A man is leaning over it. She continues to run, moving closer. The man is bent over her former professor, who is lying flat on the wooden slats, and looks to be unconscious. The hovering man has ripped open the old man's shirt. He looks up at her as she stands behind them, loudly drawing in air: *Call an ambulance, for Chrissake.*

The woman cannot think. She can hardly breathe, but keeps putting one foot in front of the other and moves as fast as she can. She tries to remember where the call-boxes are, but her thoughts fly by too quickly to be of any use. She hears an ambulance's siren; perhaps someone has already called. She continues to sprint, past the Peter Pan statue, to Bayswater road, where there are a series of telephones. She asks a passerby for some change. *Emergency*; she can barely gasp the words. A woman on the line takes the information in a deadpan, almost robotic way. When the woman is asked to identify herself she shouts, *jogger*, smashes the telephone down into its cradle, and begins running back to the bench.

Clusters of people are standing around. An ambulance and police vehicle are at the site. She pushes her way to the front of the crowd, easy to do as she is sweaty, breathing in loud gasps and people instinctively move away. They lift the man into the back of the ambulance. His shoes point to the sky.

She thinks she may be shrieking, but nobody turns to look at her, so perhaps she isn't. When she is certain she will be able to speak with a bit of composure, she asks a man next to her what happened; he has no idea; the ambulance pulls away. Although the day is warm and humid, the woman suddenly becomes cold, wraps her arms around herself and walks back toward the health club.

o

For the next several days she scans the papers for the man's obituary or an account of what happened. Had the hovering man murdered the old man, or was he trying to save him? The young man was not in the police car while the crowd was grouped around. Had another police vehicle taken him into custody as she ran to Bayswater road? Was that perhaps the siren she'd heard? Was there an altercation that scared the old man, inducing a heart attack? Despite her buying both editions of all the dailies, the man's name wasn't mentioned in any of them. The woman thinks of going to the man's home, knocking on the door and asking his family what happened—or of contacting the Hyde Park police, but she can never devise a scheme to make these plans seem feasible.

1.

HE ALWAYS DOES his laundry on Monday. For the past several weeks a woman has been coming in at the same time. She hoists her washing into a machine, sits and reads. When the washing's done, she shoves it in a dryer, sits and reads some more. It is steamy, humid in the laundromat, and the young man wonders how she can stand it. He goes out for a cigarette, she doesn't look up, and when he returns her eyes are still on the book. He finds this annoying; he'd like to ask her to keep an eye on his things while he goes to the pub a few doors down for a quick one. He has rather good luck getting women to do what he asks.

One Monday he thinks: why not invite *her* to the pub? She is surprised he is speaking to her at all, looks up from her book and says *no* in a voice that's a little irritated.

Today, though, she agrees—although he was halfway hoping she'd decline. If she'd said no, he might have been able to persuade her to watch his things, and maybe even put them in a dryer for him while he had a *couple* of pints.

She is a lecturer at university. This is what she looks like, he thinks—academic, with her dark clothes and glasses. He watches her as she pays for her pint and he guesses there's only a dozen or so years between them. She has an "I am a Lecturer at University" persona which, he guesses, she believes she needs to employ because he is younger, a student. But when she drops the pose she's funny, not stuffy like most of the faculty. He fantasizes about taking one of her courses, and her giving him a high mark whether he does the work or not.

She says: *Do you want to hear something odd?* He'd rather do the taking, but he is certain she's going to tell him nonetheless.

Several days previously, she'd met with a former professor, who also taught at university, long ago. She becomes distressed—goes on about drinks, peculiar trousers, and this man insulted a little girl near the Serpentine. The young man could have lived without the story, but pretends otherwise, is sympathetic. They finish their pints go back and do their drying.

o

He thinks about the woman at the laundromat while he and his girlfriend sit around their flat. They always do something on Sundays, but it's raining so hard they can't figure out where to go. He doesn't see what's wrong with a movie, there are plenty of theatres near any underground....He refuses to be dragged around to the shops today, and he wishes his girlfriend would turn off the classical music, or play something a little more cheerful.

He finds it strange the woman in the laundromat is so bothered by meeting the former professor. People change, people get old....He decides she can't have much of a life if she gets that upset about someone she has not seen in years.

The young man can tell every time she's seen the old geezer…she is always depressed. What's it to her if the old man's not well, or if he's gone crazy?

He knows she likes it when they leave their washing spinning around in the sudsy water and go for a pint. It's rather irresponsible, and she hardly does anything irresponsible.

o

As they drink beer the woman tells another story, about going to a knocking shop with the former professor where he removed his clothes, got into bed and played along with a television quiz show. Her story is made more odd by the flat tone of voice with which she tells it. The young man likes this story a lot more than the first, and thinks she is probably joking. He laughs, then is sorry for her—if it is true that the old bugger preferred the television to her.

He wonders how long it's been since she's had sex, and why

she told him this story. She's been looking better when she comes to the laundromat, wearing dresses and some makeup.

When their laundry is finished and he is on his way home, he considers that she might be telling him these stories so they will develop an intimacy, which will lead to their having a sexual encounter.

Back at home he goes to his girlfriend who is sitting on the couch, slides her jeans and knickers down, eases her onto the floor and performs oral sex.

o

He sometimes wakes up in the middle of the night—some dream he can't remember. He lies awake for about half an hour and drops back off to sleep. Tonight he gets to thinking about them…the woman in the laundromat is as crazy as the old man. This afternoon she was walking around Hyde Park in the pouring rain, looking for him. Sometimes it seems like she and the old man are having an affair, but why would she want to do that; she could be with someone else. He looks over at this girlfriend, is glad she is asleep. Before nodding off again he wishes the idea of an affair hadn't occurred to him for a second time.

o

They decide to have three pints each. He says: *today let's have three pints each.* He thinks she will say she can just have the one, she's got work to do after, but she doesn't. During the second pint he takes her hand in his and holds it as they talk. Halfway through the third pint, he pulls his Swiss army knife from his pocket, carves his initials into the bench they're sitting on and gives her the knife to do the same. When she is finished, he places his hand over hers and they scratch an ampersand between their initials. Their handiwork stands out blond in the dark varnished wood, and they giggle like adolescents. The barman looks over at them often, but he cannot see what they're up to. He probably thinks they are just a little drunk, and in love.

When they return to the laundromat they are suddenly uncomfortable. The young man walks home lugging his girlfriend's green laundry basket, deciding he doesn't want to jeopardize what he has.

London is full of nice and pretty women. Here are four in a row who all smile when he looks at them.

He assumes he and his girlfriend will get married. She'll dish out the ultimatum, maybe in six months, maybe a year—it depends on what happens with the other things in her life. If they go well he'll have more time.... He's ruined plenty of relationships by getting involved with other women.

He makes some tea and puts away his clothes before his girlfriend gets home.

There is a possible solution: if the woman in the laundromat asks him for sex, he'll consider it, but *she* has to do the asking and he'll do it just the once.

He puts his feet up on the coffee table. It is always good to have a cup of tea in peace. He congratulates himself for being such a rational fellow after three pints.

o

Why is she acting so differently? One thing is certain, she no longer wants to go to the pub. She again sits across from the washing machines and reads a book. He is stunned, doesn't know how to respond, goes out for a cigarette and when he comes back in sits next to her. He can't think of what to say, doesn't suggest going anywhere. She tells him she recently joined a gym.

She's become so formal, asking him which professors he likes studying with and equally dull, polite things. He watches her fold her clothes. She moves differently, with more confidence. On her way out the door she pauses, saying: *I've stopped seeing [. . . . .]* . She puts her shoulder to the glass door and pushes her way out of the door to the street, her arms encircling her laundry basket.

o

The young man sits alone in the laundromat for the next three weeks. Each time she doesn't appear he becomes angry. He thinks he should have fucked her while he had the chance.

o

She runs into the laundromat, breathless and without any laundry. He was certain she'd be back, but he pretends he doesn't care one way or the other. He tells her to calm down, and that they should go to the pub. She downs a pint in four gulps; she thinks the old professor is dead. She saw him in Hyde Park lying on a bench, a young man was near him, there was an ambulance…but not a word in the newspapers. She takes one of the young man's hands in her own and she reveals her plan: she wants him to go to the old man's house in Kensington, ring the bell and ask for him. But the young man objects. He's busy, he can't just be running over to Kensington and knocking on some old guy's door, especially since the guy's probably dead. She sighs, begins fiddling with her hair and says there's no one else she can ask. The young man sets down his pint, puts his mouth over hers, kisses her, then reaches his hand inside her jacket and squeezes her breast. While his eyes are closed two men at the bar shout: *way to go, mate.*

o

He rings the bell before stuffing the piece of paper she gave him in his pocket. He looks all around the entryway—it's typical for this area—posh, white house with a black wrought iron fence. He tries to guess how much this place would sell for. She never said the old man was well off. A boy is at the door, maybe fourteen-years-old and he asks for [.... ....] The boy says, *Just a minute*, and the young man tries to figure out what to say when the old man appears. But the person at the door is a well dressed woman in her early 50s, considerably younger than the old man. He can see she is nervous, although she's doing her best to hide it. Again he asks for [.... ....]. *He's not here.* She's angry. *When will he be back?* She slams the door in his face.

Does this confirm that the old man is dead? He'll go over it in the laundromat with her on Monday and won't forget any of the details, so he can tell her everything. She'll know what it means.

o

She usually arrives by 4:00 p.m. Maybe she has a meeting at university, or something else has kept her.

○

The young man knows she isn't coming back. Maybe he scared her off by playing with her breast in public. Maybe she ran off with the old bugger. He could have been in hospital and telephoned her. Perhaps she got him out and they disappeared together. He could find out easily enough by going to her department at university. But why should he? He did her a favor, remembered all the details to give her a good picture of the whole thing. Why should he track her down on top of it?

This place is so hot and stuffy…he goes out for a cigarette …again regrets not sleeping with the woman while he had the chance, or at least getting oral sex…He glances down at the cigarette in his left hand; he really should make a serious effort to stop smoking.

Doing laundry is quite tedious.

1.

SHE IS A weary and withdrawn woman, she thinks, staring out the window of her flat at the rain. She looks again at the piece of paper in her right hand, listing the days and times of when she is allowed to call. She has copied them from a long message left on her answering machine. She checks the time on the kitchen clock and dials. The man seems delighted to be speaking to her.

o

A man she used to know is sitting before her in a stained, out-of-date, corduroy jacket, making snide remarks about her last two books. She is relieved when he suggests something to drink, but when the alcohol enters her bloodstream the flowers on the maroon carpet look gaudy and appear to clash with the rest of the room's decor.

He goes on about an area of study that was once his field, as if it should also be hers.

He begins questioning a young girl about politics while they stroll the Serpentine. Why on earth would he do such a thing?

It's true what they say, London continues to deteriorate. It is not often apparent in the woman's day-to-day surroundings, but sometimes while waiting for the underground she notices the garbage and wrappers that used to be cleared away, the posters and announcements once placed straight and centered on the walls, and are now slapped over peeling ones, the dirt that moves on the floor under the seats as the cars rattle and bump over the tracks.

She feels a man's leg next to her own, through the cloth of her skirt, and moves to the next series of seats, gets off a stop early and walks the rest of the way home.

o

She sees the large pile of laundry stacked high in its basket and remembers it is Monday. She supposes she should haul it down to the laundromat and wonders whether the young man in jeans, white T-shirt and black leather jacket—the undergraduate uniform, will be there today, posing against the shiny silver machines, wanting her, as he undoubtedly wants all women, to find him attractive. She will continue to be obstinate, to keep her head down, her eyes on her book, will daydream and read, not looking at the young man except when he goes out to smoke. Then she will stare at his backside, his broad shoulders inside his black leather coat.

o

What should she say to this young man? Probably nothing, should probably let him drink his beer and talk—tell her about his major, his classes, his significant other. A man such as this will always have a significant other, unless he is completely psychotic, and even then there will usually be some girl putting up with it—trying to rescue him emotionally, or financially. But she is nervous, begins babbling about the man she hadn't seen in years.

Halfway through the story, she doesn't know what she is saying. Toward the story's end she begins to notice the ale's effect, and feels silly for agreeing to accompany him to the pub, and yet she wishes to take the young man's face in her hands, stroke his cheek, perhaps put her tongue in his mouth.

o

No one could erase an entire love affair from memory. Is it possible she was in love with this person fifteen odd years ago? But there is no vestige of anything, here, sitting next to her that she could have loved. This man doesn't like women, probably hates them. Was that always the case? She thinks back to her undergraduate, then graduate years. The man was rather popular at university, always came up with a clever remark or quip. A certain number of female students would not study with him because of his inherent sexism, but the woman and her friends understood the man had been born in another era and was, even all those years ago, too set in his thinking to change. It had been best to keep her distance, laugh at his jokes at the University cafeteria and learn what she could from him.

That evening she considers her hair. Perhaps he's right, she could lighten it. Curry always makes her eyes swell, feel puffy. She's glad she wears glasses, has something between her eyes and the world.

o

The woman begins to dress up a bit, wear some makeup, to see, again, what that is like. When younger she wore these things, but gave them up after they seemed pointless, and in their own way, oppressive. But there was yesterday, partly spent sitting in a darkened room in an uncomfortable chair, looking at stains on the faded pink wallpaper, while the former professor played a game on television as he sat naked in the bed.

She tells this story with more verve than the first. The young man seems to like it. As she describes the details of the room, pausing to sip from the pint, she thinks of pulling the young man's T-shirt out of his pants and running her hands over his abdomen—wondering whether his stomach would be smooth, or sinewy with muscle, and if a thin line of dark hair would run from his navel to his pubic area. Her mouth waters.

Later that evening while at the computer, working on her paper for the conference, she again fantasizes about pulling the young's man shirt from his jeans, of how he would feel in her arms, remembering the smell of the overcoat he sometimes wears—cigarettes and wool.

o

Her Wellingtons gape from her legs as she walks, allowing rain to run down her calves and settle into her socks.

She should keep trying, she can't believe the man could have really changed that much. She's just seen him when he was having bad days, when things were going badly at home. He wants something from her, but she's not sure what. Sometimes it seems like his new hobby is making her feel like a very tiny person.

At least he isn't wandering around in the rain.

o

The woman's recorded voice instructs a caller to leave a message at the sound of the tone, but the caller does not. For the eighth time in the past few days someone hangs up before the prompting signal. She refocuses her attention on her computer screen.

She remembers when laundry was a chore, nothing to be looked forward to.

It feels quite natural to have her palm enclosed in the young man's; she'd imagined if she ever touched him it would be awkward. But he holds her hand and continues talking. As he talks about his future he pulls out his Swiss army knife and digs away at the bench, cutting through the varnish and stain until his initials stand out, whitish, in the wood. He then hands her his knife, which the woman thinks a bit calculated, but she's caught up in the spirit and carves her initials under his. They make an ampersand—he places his hand over hers and they jointly hold the knife as if they were cutting cake.

Back at home while putting her laundry away she marvels that she is still able to feel that degree of desire. She thought it was something that was drying up now that she was closing in on her late thirties. She did think it somewhat strange that she wasn't attracted to anyone in all of London, save for a few men she happened to see on the tube, or in a shop, or theatre lobby. The men she encountered in her social circle—at receptions, or at parties all seemed to charge up to her and deliver monologues about themselves, where they were publishing, or where their next reading or lecture was going to be. It was easy to spot the ones that had been single for a long time—they spoke a strange array of lines, things they'd probably read in men's magazines, the objective to get a woman into bed. The effect was especially disconcerting coming from intellectuals who otherwise had a strong command of language.

o

She supposes her odd friendship with the young man is not inappropriate—as long as she does not get sexually involved with him.

o

She was making a fool of herself, this she can now see. She must find another place to do her laundry. The woman is now merely polite to the young man, who seems startled by her new attitude. She is stronger, both physically and emotionally. The physical exercise has also helped her see things more clearly, has helped to clear away any film or haze from her mind.

o

Could it be that someone she knew just died in a public park, more or less before her eyes? She is unable to concentrate on anything she must do.

o

As she kisses the young man she feels the muscles in her pelvis and abdomen softening. He smiles through half-closed eyes and his hand closes over her breast.

o

She thinks her plans and ideas sensible, rational, but several days later, she believes them completely unsound. This is why she made herself stop caring what happened to her former professor, or whether or not he is still alive. But this note. One of them is trying to draw her back in, trying to draw her back to the repetitions—back and forth to the laundromat—back and forth to the bench, spinning on the same point in her life, over and again.

The note reads:

> Please help me! I'm in a place in Hampstead. 49 Greenaway Gardens. Please help me!

A practical joke by a miffed young man used to getting what he wants? A cry for help from a sick old man put away by his family because he is an inconvenience? People play jokes all the time. People are locked away all the time.

The following morning she gets out her A to Z and looks up Greenaway Gardens. It is near Finchley Road underground.

The tube is fairly empty this late in the morning, just a few lone men and women reading books, newspapers, or staring vacantly at a map of the stops above the seats.

Finchley road has many cars but is surprisingly devoid of pedestrians. She finds Frognal Lane, then Greenaway Gardens. It is a residential area as she suspected. Number 49 is near the end, a two story house surrounded by a fieldstone wall. There is an arched wrought iron gate leading inside. She rings the buzzer and waits. When no one comes out she presses the buzzer several more times. Through an upstairs window she feels someone's eyes on her, but looks up and sees nothing, not the movement of a curtain, nor a figure. She holds her finger on the buzzer for a long time, hoping that whoever is inside will become sufficiently annoyed to come out and see what she wants. No one does. The woman looks all around to see if anyone is watching from the windows of adjacent houses, but the panes are empty, and no one is coming up the street. She cannot believe what she is doing—climbing the wall, using stones as toeholds and pulling herself up by grasping the wrought iron gate, now straddling the wall and giving a final look around before dropping down to the other side.

She hopes there is no dog on the property, but she probably would have heard one by now, and she walks around the house before going up to the front door, thinking that what she finds might offer a clue to what kind of people live here. There is a garden that is well-tended, otherwise nothing to give her any information about the residents. Discouraged, she walks around to the front of the house and aggressively knocks on the door. From a downstairs window she glimpses someone staring at her from behind a curtain. She cannot tell the gender. *Hello*, she shouts. *Hello! Please answer!* She goes to a ground floor window and bangs on it, calling out the old man's name. Has she gone too far, given whoever is inside reason to call the police? What will she say if police cars arrive—she, a university professor who is trespassing, annoying or frightening someone who does not want to speak to her, or is being prevented? She is glad she remembered to put the note in her purse. Maybe the police would take down a report, make whoever it is open the door.

The woman does not hear any sirens. She halfway expected 49 to be a nursing home, but an attendant would either have answered or chased her off by now.

How many are inside, just a lone person who went from upstairs to down to better watch her movements, or are there more hidden away, creeping about?

The gate opens easily from the inside and she lets herself out, not knowing what else to do, and from the street stares at the house, its windows, but there is no movement. She turns to rewalk her steps to the underground.

At Bond St. station where she changes trains she is nearly floored by recognition, registers that the young man is exiting three cars down—or is he? She was not expecting to see him, yet he was on her mind at Greenaway Gardens, so she could be projecting. If it turns out to be him and they can speak, his behavior will answer a lot of questions, no matter what actually comes out of his mouth.

With the thick human wall that always moves through Bond St. it takes her forever to get to the escalator.

She races to the main floor of the station, where throngs come and go, but with the bobbing bodies she cannot get a good enough look to know for certain if it was the young man, if he is conspiring.

○ ○ ○

The woman returns home, finds the note and flings it into the waste paper basket. An hour or so later she retrieves it, smoothes it out and places it on her desk where it sits, a perverse origami. In the early afternoon she balls it up and lobs it into the trash, pleased with her aim—only to fish it out again. She tears it up and disposes of the pieces, one by one, into the basket. As evening approaches she tapes it back together, a small, damaged sculpture of her chagrin and embarrassment—but also representing a spark of intrigue in an otherwise predictable life.

Enough, she thinks. There must be other types of diversion besides being insulted on benches, having breasts fondled in public, or being fooled by spurious notes. This time she takes a scissors, cuts up the tape and paper, places the pieces in the palm of her hand, goes into the bathroom and flushes them down the toilet.

Toilets, though, are not meant to dispose of such thick paper and as she returns to the living room some of the pieces float to the surface, where they are slowly rotating in the gently undulating water.

The apartment feels claustrophobic and the woman needs to get away. Without planning a destination she begins walking, finally entering an underground station and boarding the first train that stops. Many people have just gotten off work, the car is very crowded and there are no places to sit. She notes they are headed west, and after several stops that results in the car filling to even greater capacity, she gets off at Hyde Park Corner. A walk in the park will probably do her good, and she begins to stride down the paths, which are still wet from a late afternoon shower.

Although she knows it will depress her, she traverses the paths, moving in the direction of the bench. From a distance she sees it is deserted, but most of the benches she's passed have been empty, as the light is fading.

The woman stands in front of the bench, looking at all its defects and imperfections—the wear and tear from all those who have sat there, the words and scratches cut into the wood, the deterioration from the elements. She feels anxious, is irritated with herself for her irrationality and forces herself to sit, to sit quietly, to feel her back and buttocks against the slats, her boots on the grass.

All over London many recently buried bodies lie in various cemeteries, and one of them may be his, already beginning to decompose, or perhaps his body is lying in a family plot in another part of England. It could be that his remains were scattered from a small boat on the sea, near one of the villages, by somber family members in dark clothing. The possibility exists too that the man sits in a room in a dwelling somewhere in the city, or somewhere in the countryside, still coherent enough to know that his body or mind has betrayed him, that he has been trapped by one or both entities, and there is nothing she can do.

And elsewhere today, in a pub, classroom, or out on the street, the young man is seeing himself favorably reflected in the eyes of some of the several million girls and women who make their home here—has already begun to learn that their first unbridled glint of desire is the most unconditional love or affection he will ever receive, before any make his acquaintance and their spark of hope begins to fade.

It has grown dark without her paying attention. The woman jumps up, begins walking as fast as she can. A minute or two later she is almost running. There is barely a star visible and she's trying to keep close to the occasional wrought iron lamp at the edge of the path, although they do not throw much light. It is not a good idea for anyone to be alone in a city park at night and she is afraid.

The woman suddenly veers left, choosing a path she thinks might lead back to a city street, but although she knows the park well, she has not visited it for some time and it looks so different in the darkness, much larger, disorienting. She wants to run but knows she shouldn't because if she is to come across someone it will be a sure giveaway of her out-of-control anxiety. Still using a half-walking, half-running cadence that causes her to lope and hinders her speed, she continues in the same direction—unsure whether or not this is really a way out.

—Penngrove, California, 1996-2000

Cydney Chadwick is the author of seven other titles. She is the recipient of a Gertrude Stein Award in Innovative American Poetry and a creative writing fellowship from the California Arts Council. She lives in the countryside of Penngrove, California, which is about fifty miles north of San Francisco.

Cover artist Andrew Bick was born in 1963. He lives in London and exhibits in Europe and the U.S.A.

Other Pivotal Prose Titles:

Benching With Virgil by Gad Hollander
The Big Lie by Mark Wallace